The Kid's Guide To

BELLA

The Bichon Frisé

Written by A.J. Richards
Illustrated by Rayah Jaymes

The Kid's Guide to: Bella The Bichon Frise
Copyright 2014 by A.J. Richards and Rayah Jaymes

ISBN-13: 9781497377448
ISBN-10: 1497377447

Disclaimer: The information in this book does not replace a consultation with a veterinarian and/or a behavior consultant and may not be used to diagnose or treat any conditions in your dog. Dog training is not without risks. When in doubt, consult a professional dog trainer or canine behaviorist. A.J Richards cannot guarantee that your dog will instantly start to behave. Like anything in life, dog training requires work. Any issues that arise would depend on too many factors beyond our control, such as: The amount of time you are willing to invest in training your dog, your ability to apply what you have learned and the possibility that your dog may have a rare genetic or health condition affecting it's behavior. A.J Richards cannot guarantee any method will work for you and is not liable in any case of sickness, injury, or death.

Book Cover and Design by
Vermilion Chameleon Illustration and Design
www.vcartist.com

A special thanks to Carolyn Moore.
I could not have done this without you.
A.J.

Super big thanks to Miguel for your patience and love
while I created my labors of joy.
R.J

3

This Book Belongs To:

_____

Your Name

_____

Your Dog's Name

Hello! My name is Bella.
I am a Bichon Frise. Would you like to hear my story?

When I was a puppy, all I ever wanted was to be happy.
My Mom and Dad told me one day a family would come and
take me away to live in a new home.
I did not understand why I would have to leave.

"Bella," my Mom licked my head, "all puppies grow up with a new
family so they can make them happy. It is what you were born to do.
Dogs are people's best friends."

How exciting, I thought. I love people. Mom smiled,
"Bichons like to make people smile."

She said, "Bichons are **bouncy** and kind.
Many years ago, bichons had very fun jobs.
They did tricks in the **circus** and at **fairs**,
so people would laugh and smile.
They helped **blind** people.
They **guided** them when they walked,
so they would not get hurt or lost."
I knew I was born to make my new family smile,
but I would need their help.

I have **3** brothers and **2** sisters. We all lived in France. They told us we will go to good homes with families that will take care of us. One by one, my brothers and sisters found their new homes in
Egypt, Greece, Italy, Spain, and Turkey.
All of these countries surround the Mediterranean Sea.

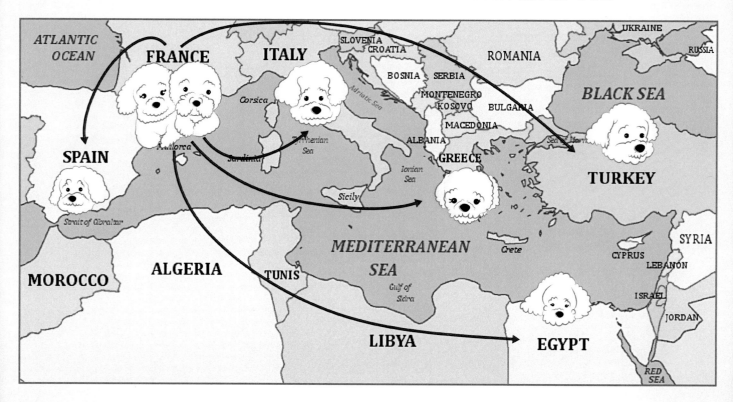

I would travel the farthest to live with my new family.
My Mom and Dad told me, "They live in the United States."
They kissed me goodbye and I started my new adventure.

I sailed in a boat, across the sea, in search of my new family. The Captain of the boat softly patted my head and scratched behind my ears, always saying, "Your new family will live in **1** of **50** states. When you go live with them make sure you show them all of the tricks you can do. You are a very special dog."
I couldn't wait to live with my new family,
but I would never forget the Captain.
He was so nice to me.

Where do you live?

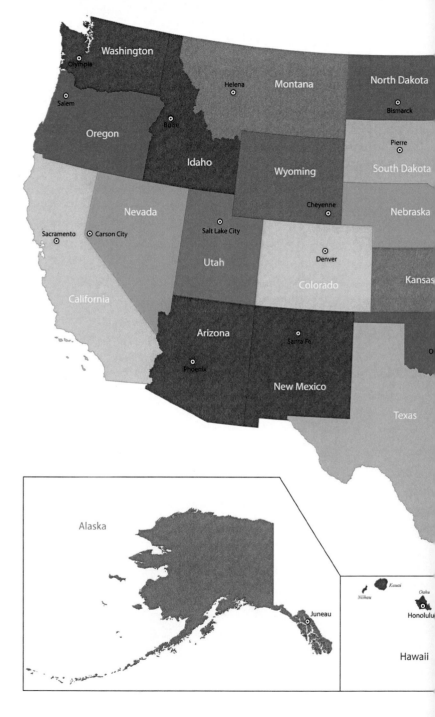

Minnesota
Saint Paul ⊙

Wisconsin
Madison ⊙

Michigan
Lansing ⊙

Maine

Vermont
Augusta ⊙
Montpelier ⊙

New Hampshire
Concord ⊙
Boston ⊙

Albany ⊙
New York

Massachusetts

Providence ⊙
Rhode Island

Hartford ⊙
Connecticut

Iowa
Des Moines ⊙

Illinois
Springfield ⊙

Indiana
Indianapolis ⊙

Ohio
Columbus ⊙

Pennsylvania
Harrisburg ⊙

Trenton ⊙
New Jersey

Annapolis ⊙
Dover ⊙
Delaware

Maryland

Washington, D.C.

Lincoln ⊙

Topeka ⊙

Jefferson City ⊙

Missouri

Kentucky
Frankfort ⊙

West Virginia
Charleston ⊙

Richmond ⊙

Virginia

Raleigh ⊙

Oklahoma
Oklahoma City ⊙

Arkansas
Little Rock ⊙

Tennessee
Nashville ⊙

North Carolina

Columbia ⊙

South Carolina

Mississippi
Jackson ⊙

Alabama
Montgomery ⊙

Atlanta ⊙

Georgia

Louisiana
Baton Rouge ⊙

Tallahassee ⊙

Austin ⊙

Florida

Can you find it?

Molokai
Maui
Lanai
Kahoolawe
Hawaii

I want to live with your family!
Please listen very carefully so you can learn how
to take care of me.

I will be very dirty from my boat ride and I like to keep my fur white and clean.

I will need a bath at least **1** day in each month.

There are **12** months in **1** year.
Can you say the months with me?

January	July
February	August
March	September
April	October
May	November
June	December

Good Job!

I might whine and try to run away when you wash and brush me.
So to keep me happy, please talk to me softly and tell me,
"Everything will be okay."

Be Gentle.

Count with me!

This is how much I should weigh.
My new family will have to help me be healthy.
They will never feed me too much!

Hmmm....
But no more
than 20.

Do you have a **measuring cup** in your home?
I am a puppy, so my new family can only feed me **1/4** of a cup each
of these times during the day:
once for breakfast, once for lunch, once for dinner, and once
before bedtime.

1 CUP
3/4 CUP
1/2 CUP
1/4 CUP

DOGGY BITES

BELLA

My Dad promised, "Your new family will only feed you dog food and treats from the pet store."
I have never been to a pet store. I love new places and food, but too much food can make me sick and unhealthy.
I will eat anything people give me even if it is bad for me.

Dogs cannot have certain foods.
These are some of the foods dogs cannot eat.
Please say them with me.

CHOCOLATE

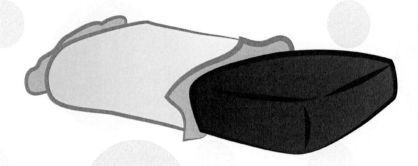

APPLE SEEDS

GRAPES

AVOCADO

TOMATO

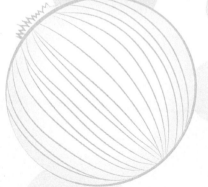

ONION

Do you remember when I told you, when I am puppy, I eat **4** times a day?

When I grow up, I only want to eat breakfast and dinner.

Dry dog food is better for my teeth. If I will not eat it, then add a little bit of water to make it soft.

You can give me dog treats when you are teaching me tricks or when I do something nice.

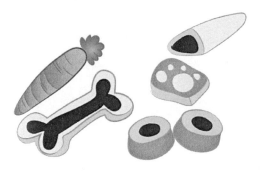

Take me on **1** walk every day.
Do NOT let me walk in front of you and pull you with the **leash**.
I might not like it at first, but I will be much happier if you make me walk next to you. Please teach me how to do this.

There are lots of smart people that can show you the best way to walk me.
They are called Dog Trainers.
They can teach our family lots of stuff to help us take better care of each other.

I like fresh water to drink. Drinking water means you will have to take me outside on a **leash** to go to the bathroom.

I do NOT want you to be mad at me if I go to the bathroom in the house.

It may take me more time than other dogs to potty train so please be **patient** with me. Keep a close eye on me. I might have to go to the bathroom if...

I am sniffing by doors,
I am spinning in circles,
I am running in and out of rooms.

If you have friends over please don't let them chase me!
Please do NOT tease me or move too fast.
Please do not pull on my tail or poke me.
I will be scared and I might bite them. I don't want to do this.

BE CAREFUL!
I might bite if I am growling, if I am backing up or if
I am showing my teeth.

These are some important **manners** we should learn:
when someone new is in our home, ask an adult for help
so we are not alone.
Ask our **guest** to squat down, turn a little to the side, and
pat their legs and wait until I come over to say, "Hi."
When I'm ready to make new friends,
I will sniff our guests and lean towards them.

Please help me be kind. Ask your friends to be nice and use their
manners in our home.
People and dogs both have to learn manners.

Best friends help each other. I am your best friend now.
I will cuddle with you when you are sad.
I will kiss you when you are kind. I live to make you smile.
Every day I am with our family is the best day of my life.

I am so happy you learned how to take care of me. I hope you love me as much as I love you.
Thank you!

Love, Bella

GLOSSARY

Bichon Frisé: A small dog with curly white fur and a tail that curves over its back.

Blind: Cannot see through his or her eyes.

Bouncy: Happy and energetic.

Circus: A traveling show, where a group of acrobats, clowns, and animals perform for people in different cities and town.

Countries: Lands where people live.

Dog Trainer: A person who teaches dogs how to act around people and other animals.

Fairs: Educational and entertaining games, music, rides, and contests in cities and towns.

Gentle: Quiet and calm with touch and voice.

Growling: A low or harsh rumbling sound that comes from the throat of a dog when he or she is mad.

GLOSSARY

Guest: A person or animal invited to someone's home or activity.

Guided: Showing the way to someone.

Leash: A strap or cord used to guide or keep a dog or other animal under control. Use this to keep a dog and people safe.

Manners: A polite way of behaving towards others.

Map: Names and pictures of the land where people live.

Measuring Cup: A cup used to help you pick the right amount of food or liquid.

Patient: Able to wait without getting mad.

Tease: Making fun of or pretending to give someone something and then taking it away.

Train: To teach a skill or behavior by giving directions and practicing over a period of time.

Educational Websites

American Dog Trainers Network

http://www.inch.com/~dogs/housebreaking.html

American Kennel Club

http://www.akc.org/breeds/bichon_frise/index.cfm

Kids Health

http://kidshealth.org/kid/watch/out/dogs.html#

Bichon Frisé Club of America Inc.

http://bichon.org/CareFeeding.htm

IXL

http://www.ixl.com/math/grades

Educational Websites

Cesar Milan
http://www.cesarsway.com/

Janet Wall's How to Love Your Dog:
A Kid's Guide to Dog Care
http://www.loveyourdog.com/

Bark Busters: Home Dog Training
http://www.barkbusters.com/

Author

A.J.Richards, from an early age, has been surrounded by family pets: dogs, cats, horses, deer, hamsters, gerbils and many others to name a few. Also, she had numerous shelter pets throughout her adulthood.
She earned her Bachelor's degree in American Literature and a Master's in Public Adminisration, all while working with at-risk youth for a Nebraska non-profit.
She now lives in Berkeley, California.

Illustrator

Rayah Jaymes is an illustrator, chef and musician that comes from an incredibly large multicultral family which continues to inspire her art and story telling.
She aspires to illustrate many more books that educate children and their parents about the diverse world around them and how they can make it better everyday in everything they do.

Find her and more of her books at www.vcartist.com

www.dogbooksforkids.com

More Books from A Puppy's New Home

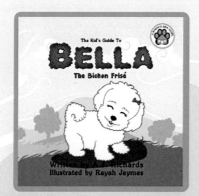

Coming Soon

Made in the USA
San Bernardino, CA
05 March 2018